I SURVIVED A SKELETON!

by Christy Webster
illustrated by Alan Batson

A RANDOM HOUSE PICTUREBACK® BOOK

RANDOM HOUSE 🏠 NEW YORK

rhcbooks.com
ISBN 978-0-593-48429-6 (trade) – ISBN 978-0-593-48430-2 (ebook)
Printed in the United States of America
10 9 8 7 6 5 4 3 2 1

It began deep in the caves. I had been mining down there for so long, I didn't know whether it was day or night, or what could be lurking around any corner. I tried my best to keep the way lit up, but . . .

Many things found me! **Skeletons!** Each aiming a pointy arrow right at me.

I'm Sam, by the way.　　　And that's a spawner nearby.

Lucky for me, it was daytime.
As I hurried through the caves and into
the light, the skeletons chased me,
catching fire in the sun, one by one.

If skeletons were wandering around this open space with bows and arrows, they wouldn't have to get close to me to hurt me. I needed more gear. And I would need to make it myself.

I had some spare iron and wood, so I started crafting.

That night, I was ready with my new shield and iron armor. I hiked across the snowy mountains until I heard the telltale clanking of bones.

What I saw looked just like a skeleton, but even spookier than the ones in the caves. It wore loose rags on its bony body. It was a **stray**! Worse than that, it was about to shoot!

I braced myself. *TWANG!*
The arrow lodged in my shield. I was safe!

I took my chance and attacked! After I defeated the stray in battle, I found its bow and some arrows on the ground.

I nocked an arrow and pulled back. No wonder the skeletons carried bows: I felt powerful.

WHOOSH!

Another arrow flew past my head.

Perhaps I was powerful, but it would probably still be better to find a safer place to experiment.

So I built my observation tower high above a nearby field. Then it started to rain.

From up high,
I could see skeletons.
I could see creepers,
zombies, and spiders, too.
They didn't mind the rain
at all. Then . . .

ZAP!

I couldn't believe my eyes. At the far end of the field, lightning struck the ground!

The storm let up, and daylight started to show over the horizon. I peered across the field at the spot where the lightning had touched down. I thought I could see something—something I had never seen before.

With my shield in tow, I hurried past the burning mobs and found a horse. It wasn't just any horse— it was a skeleton horse!

I wanted to get a little closer, but when I did—

ZZZZAAP!

Another lightning bolt hit. I looked up at the sky, but the storm was long gone. The sky was blue. When I looked back, I saw four skeleton horses—with four skeletons riding on them!

These skeletons didn't burn in the sun. Their shining enchanted helmets protected them. They had enchanted bows, too.

I knew I was outnumbered. I hurried away to safety— and tried not to get hit by any of the arrows flying past me! Luckily, I sprinted so fast that I left the skeleton horsemen far behind. I could see them in the distance when I was back on my tower.

I didn't have much practice with my new bow, but it was worth a try. I nocked an arrow, aimed, and let go. . . .

Bull's-eye!

Advancement Made!
Take Aim

Soon the skeleton horses
were riderless, and surrounded
with enchanted loot for the
taking.

Even though the horses looked
just as spooky as their riders, they
didn't seem to want to hurt me.
Suddenly, I had a great idea.

I scurried back across the field, through the snowy mountains, and into my cave. With my new gear, I was ready to take on the skeleton spawner.

I defeated the skeletons and I found what I was looking for: a saddle.

Now I felt like I could take on anything!

Another adventure awaits. . . .